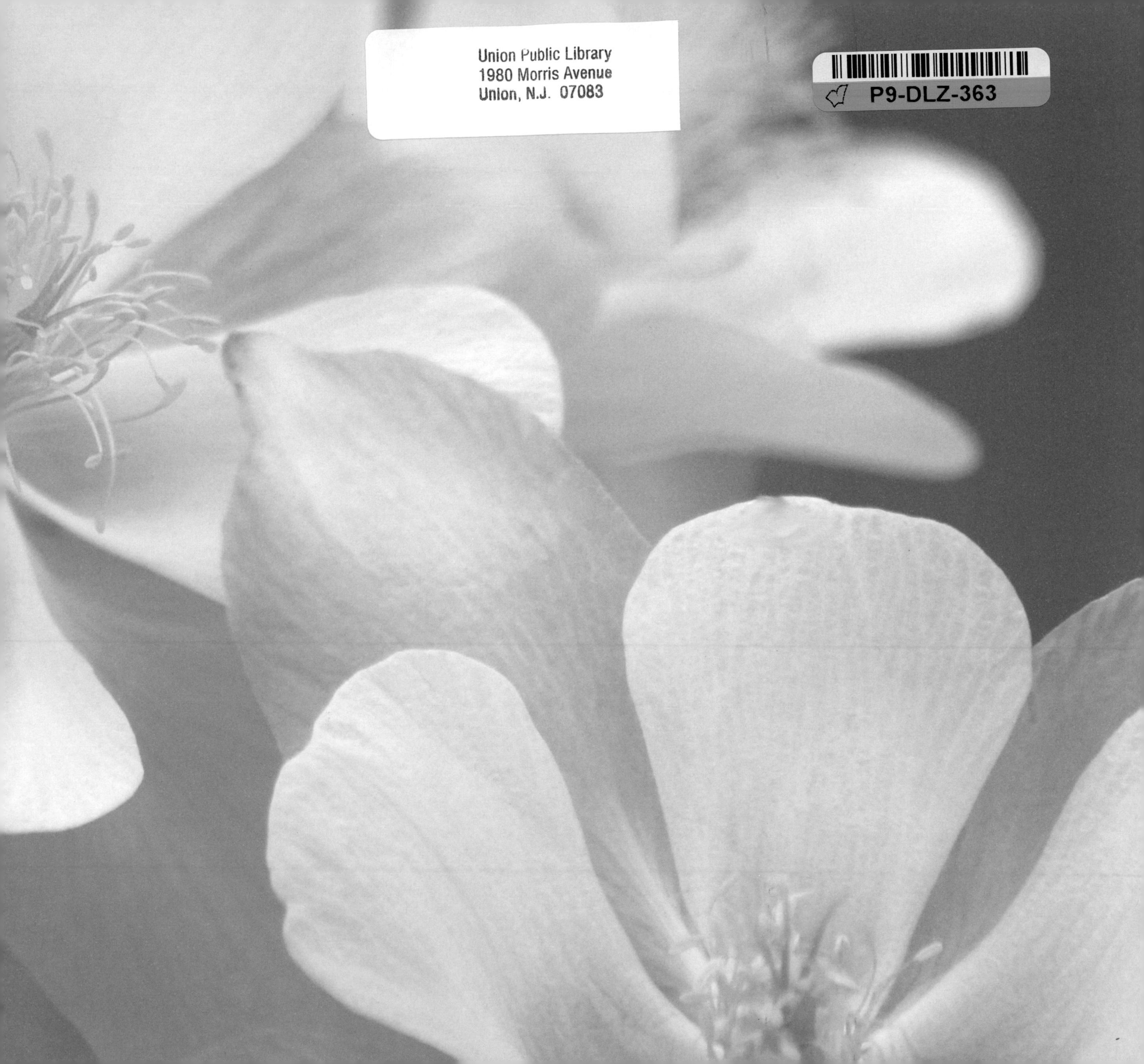

Looking Closely

inside
the
Garden

FRANK SERAFINI

Kids Can Press

Look very closely.

What do you see?

A stained-glass window?
A jigsaw puzzle?
What could it be?

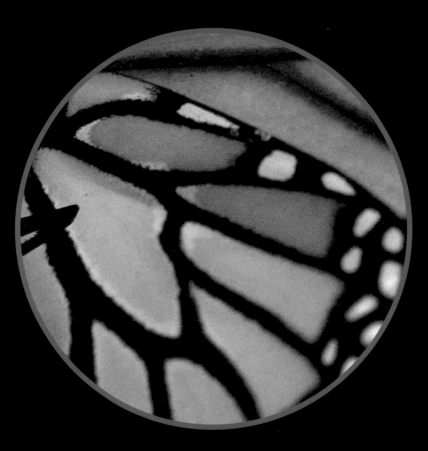

It's a Monarch Butterfly.

In autumn, when the weather grows cold, monarch butterflies fly south to Mexico and Central America. They follow the same path every year.

At the end of their long journey, monarch butterflies lay their eggs on milkweed plants. When caterpillars hatch from the eggs, they munch on milkweed leaves until their bodies are large enough to form a smooth chrysalis. Eventually, they emerge as butterflies.

Look very closely.

What do you see?

A pirate's hook?
A purple ribbon?
What could it be?

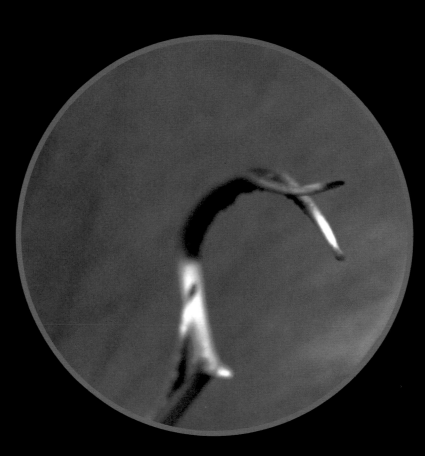

It's a Princess Flower.

Like most plants, the princess flower attracts both people and insects with its colorful blooms and lovely scents. This shrub is also called a glory bush because of its bright, enormous flowers.

The princess flower's velvety purple petals invite hungry bees and butterflies to draw near. As the insects feed, the flower's pollen rubs off on their bodies. Insects spread pollen as they visit different plants in the garden. When pollen from one flower gets mixed into another flower, a seed is created.

Look very  closely.

What do you see?

A pair of chopsticks?
An alligator's nose?
What could it be?

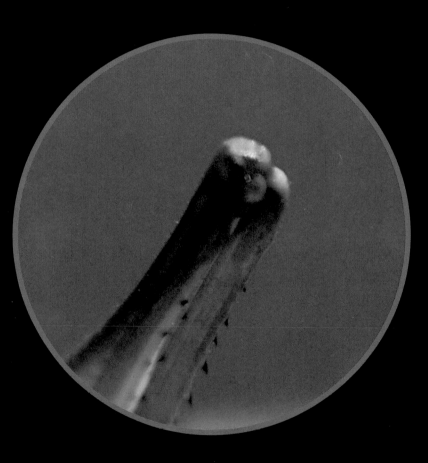

It's a Mormon Cricket.

The Mormon cricket lives in fields and meadows, where there is plenty of food. One story says these insects got their name after swarming a Mormon farming community. The farmers' crops were saved when gulls swooped in and ate the pests.

In fact, the Mormon cricket is not a cricket, but a katydid. Katydids are named for the noise they make, which sounds like "katy-did, katy-didn't." They "sing" by rubbing their wings together.

Look very closely.

What do you see?

Rubber tubes?
Octopus tentacles?
What could it be?

It's a Common Earthworm.

Earthworms live in most warm climates around the globe. They can be shorter than 3 cm (1 in.) or grow up to 3 m (10 ft.) long. These worms are also called "night crawlers" because they slither out of the ground at night, usually after it rains.

Earthworms live in the soil and eat bits of dirt and organic matter, such as rotting leaves. Gardeners like earthworms because they leave their droppings in the soil. Like plant food, earthworm droppings help plants and flowers grow.

Look very closely.

What do you see?

Dark chocolate?
Tree bark?
What could it be?

It's a Roman Snail.

Snails live almost everywhere in the world. Most snails can be found in or near the water, but the roman snail lives on land. It has eyes on the ends of its tentacles and glides slowly along the ground on a strong, slimy foot.

Snails secrete minerals that form a shell around their bodies. These spiral-shaped shells protect the snail. When threatened, snails hide inside their shells until it's safe to come out again.

Look very  closely.

What do you see?

Flower petals?
Bananas?
What could it be?

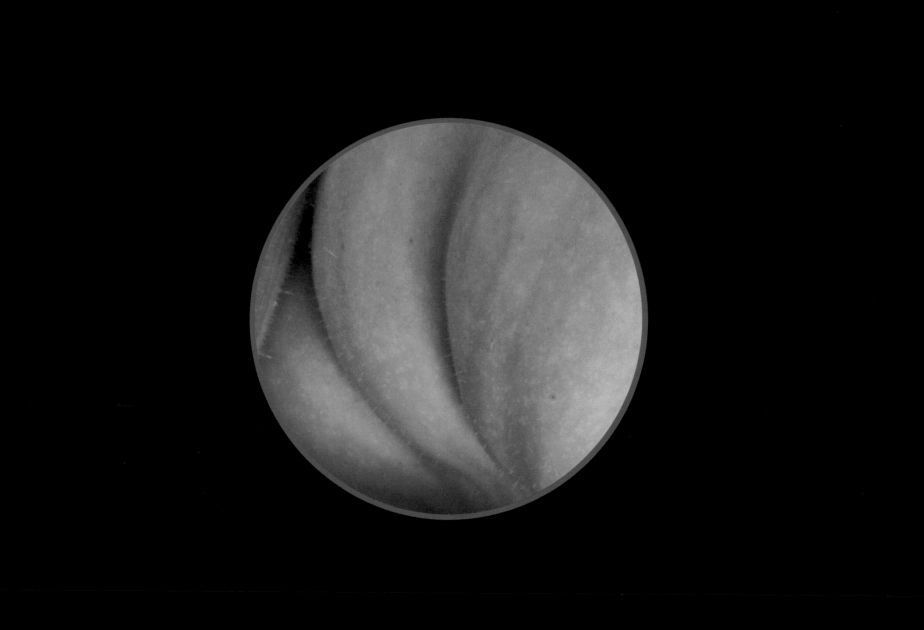

It's a Common Pumpkin.

Pumpkins were first grown thousands of years ago in North America. They are squash fruits, or gourds, that sprout on vines along the ground. Long dimples, called "ribs," support the fruit as it gets bigger.

You may have carved pumpkins into jack-o'-lanterns for Halloween. Maybe you have even roasted pumpkin seeds for a snack! People also cook the insides of pumpkins to make soup, bread and, of course, pumpkin pie.

Look very closely.

What do you see?

A tongue?
A sponge?
What could it be?

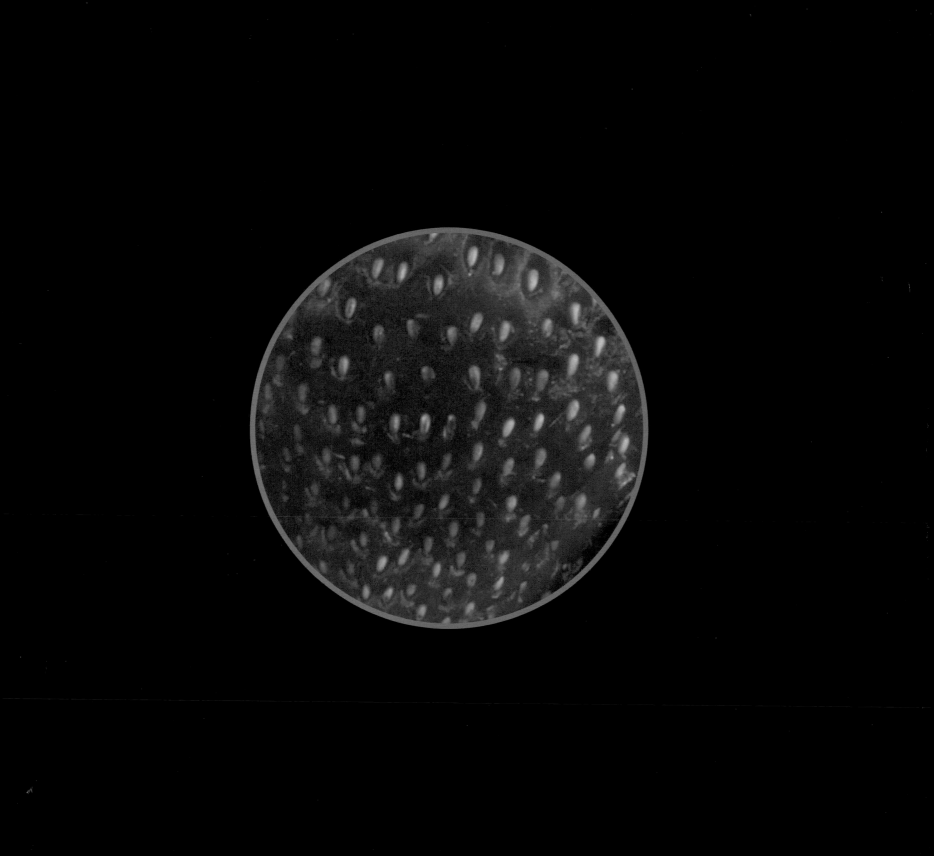

It's a Strawberry.

The strawberry is the only fruit that has its seeds on the outside. But seeds aren't the only way to grow new strawberry plants. Strawberry plants send out thin shoots, or runners, along the ground. When these take root, new strawberry plants will sprout.

Some kinds of strawberries grow in the wild, but most are harvested on farms. Strawberries are sweet and also very healthy. They contain lots of vitamins and are used in making jam and ice cream.

Look very closely.

What do you see?

A diamond necklace?
The Milky Way?
What could it be?

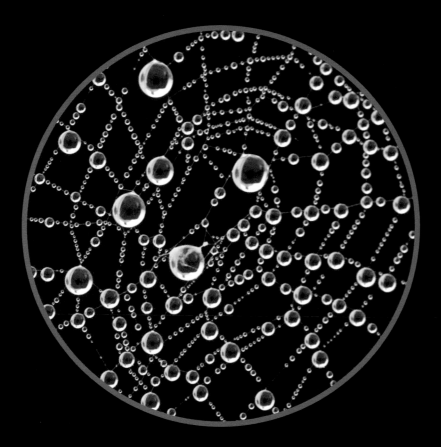

It's a Spider Web.

Spiders spin webs to trap insects for food. They weave their webs with silken threads made inside their bodies. Spiders also use this sticky thread to spin egg sacs that protect their eggs.

The most common type of web is an orb web, which looks like a bicycle wheel. It takes an adult spider about an hour to spin a full web. Large spiders spin bigger webs, and small spiders spin smaller ones.

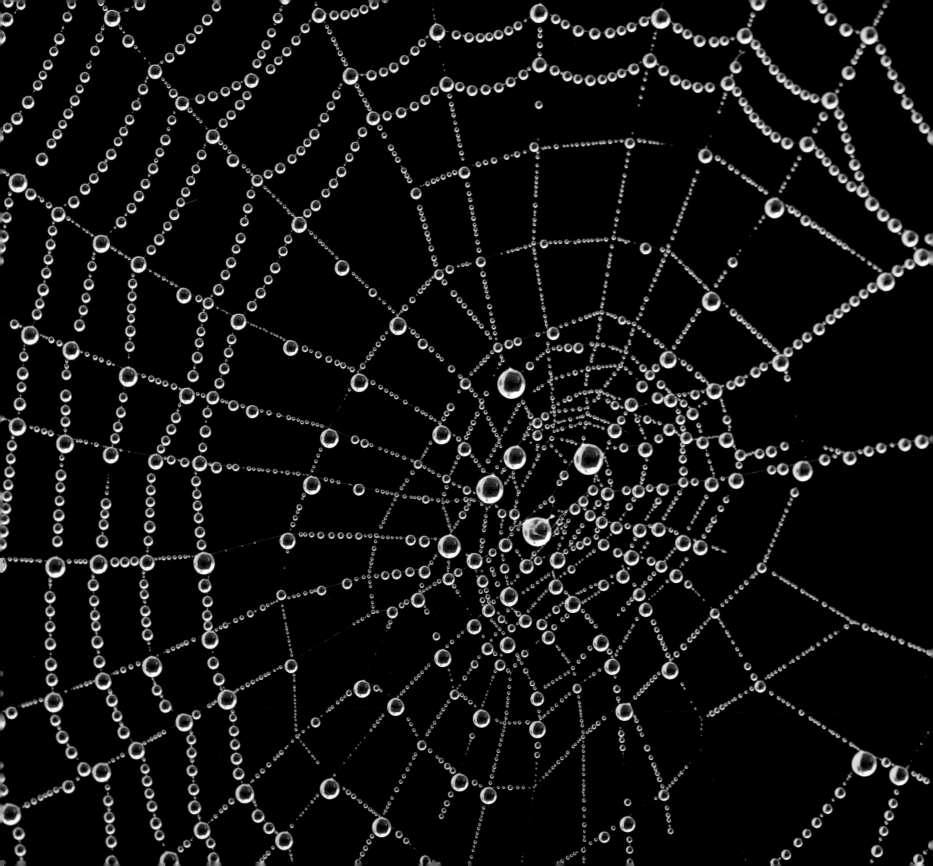

Look very closely.

What do you see?

Golden hair?
Spaghetti?
What could it be?

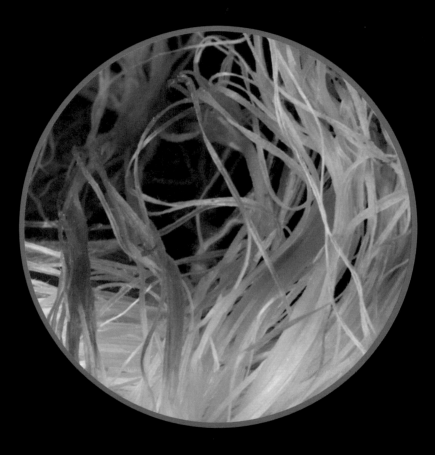

It's an Ear of Corn.

Humans have been eating corn for thousands of years. Early native peoples called it "maize." It was first harvested in South and Central America. Today, corn is also used to feed animals and make car fuel.

It takes all summer long for corn to grow and be ready to eat. The average ear of corn has over 800 kernels lined up in 16 rows. Each kernel is the seed for a new corn plant. It can also be popped into popcorn!

This book is dedicated to my mother, Dolores Ann Serafini, for tending our family garden and helping us to grow into the people we are

Photographer's Note

Photographers pay attention to things that most people overlook or take for granted. I can spend hours wandering along the shore, through the forest, across the desert or in my garden, looking for interesting things to photograph. My destination is not a place, but rather a new way of seeing.

It takes time to notice things. To be a photographer, you have to slow down and imagine in your "mind's eye" what the camera can capture. Ansel Adams said you could discover a whole life's worth of images in a six-square-foot patch of Earth. In order to do so, you have to look very closely.

By creating the images featured in this series of picture books, I hope to help people attend to nature, to things they might have normally passed by. I want people to pay attention to the world around them, to appreciate what nature has to offer, and to begin to protect the fragile environment in which we live.

Kids Can Press acknowledges the financial support of the Government of Ontario, through the Ontario Media Development Corporation's Ontario Book Initiative.

Published in Canada by	Published in the U.S. by
Kids Can Press Ltd.	Kids Can Press Ltd.
29 Birch Avenue	2250 Military Road
Toronto, ON M4V 1E2	Tonawanda, NY 14150

www.kidscanpress.com

Edited by Karen Li
Designed by Julia Naimska
Printed and bound in China

This book is smyth sewn casebound.

CM 08 0 9 8 7 6 5 4 3 2 1

Library and Archives Canada Cataloguing in Publication

Serafini, Frank
Looking closely inside the garden / Frank Serafini.

(Looking closely)
ISBN 978-1-55453-210-0

1. Plants—Juvenile literature. 2. Garden animals—Juvenile literature.

I. Title. II. Title: Into the garden. III. Series: Looking closely (Toronto, Ont.)

QH541.5.G37S47 2008   j578.75'54   C2007-905566-4

Kids Can Press is a CORUS™ Entertainment company